D1095584

COBWEB CASTLE

JAN WAHL

DRAWINGS BY EDWARD GOREY

Pomegranate Kids®

Published by PomegranateKids®, an imprint of Pomegranate Communications, Inc.
19018 NE Portal Way, Portland OR 97230
800 227 1428 | www.pomegranate.com

Pomegranate Europe Ltd.
Unit 1, Heathcote Business Centre, Hurlbutt Road
Warwick, Warwickshire CV34 6TD, UK
[+44] 0 1926 430111 | sales@pomeurope.co.uk

To learn about new releases and special offers from Pomegranate, please visit www.pomegranate.com and sign up for our e-mail newsletter. For all other queries, see "Contact Us" on our home page.

This edition first published by Pomegranate Communications, Inc., 2014.

This product is in compliance with the Consumer Product Safety Improvement Act of 2008 (CPSIA).

Library of Congress Control Number: 2013950068

ISBN 978-0-7649-6801-3

Pomegranate Catalog No. A231
Designed by Carey Hall

Printed in China
23 22 21 20 19 18 17 16 15 14 10 9 8 7 6 5 4 3 2 1

To
Bradley Gillaugh
and to
Aase Malmkjaer

Flemming Flinders, who worked in a greengrocery
selling turnips, potatoes, onions, and squash,
stood at the counter, dreaming and
reading fairy-tales. He wondered if he, too,
mightn't find fame and fortune
somewhere out in the world?

So one day he put on his best suit
and said good-bye to Nisse, the store cat,
and tied to a long stick a kerchief
into which he planned to put the gold he found.
Happily he set off down the road.

He had only walked a mile or two
when he saw an old lady with a
wart on her big nose. Her name was Drukamella.
He believed she must be a witch.
Therefore he asked, “Can you tell me
how I can grow richer than ever before
in my life?”
She stood there, tapping her foot.
She was late getting somewhere already.

“What was that qucstion again?”
Drukamella asked, looking at her watch.
“Can you tell me how I can grow richer
than ever before in my life?” he
repeated, louder.
At last she said, wanting to get rid of him, “All right.
You go down the road, immediately,
till you come to a tree with two crows sitting in it.
If you speak to the right crow,
he probably will tell you what you must do.”

So Flemming Flinders went down the road
till he came to the tree
with two crows sitting in it.
“This must be the tree,” he said.
“But which crow is the right crow?” he wondered.
One was on an upper branch,
and one was on a lower branch.
“Hello,” he said to one. “A nice afternoon, isn’t it?”
However, it wasn’t the right crow, and it didn’t
say anything.

So back Flemming Flinders went down the road,
until he found Drukamella hurrying over
a hill, almost out of sight.
"What do I do now?" he asked.
"Why don't you try speaking to the other crow?"
she snapped—

so this is what he did.
And that crow answered, "A *very* nice afternoon."
Then the crow flew down over his wide-brimmed hat,
and sat on his hat.
"Watch closely," the crow whispered in his ear,
"and I'll show you something."

(It was a talking crow, which
had escaped from a vaudeville theater.
Signor Monteverdi, who owned the crow,
was looking for it desperately with a net.)

Flemming and the crow walked on till
they came to a thickly tangled, spooky forest.
In the middle of the forest was a lake,
and at the side of the lake there lay a rowboat.

Flemming Flinders got in the rowboat,
with the crow on his hat,
and rowed out into the water.
Far out in thc lake he saw an island,
and on the island there was a huge house.
“Cobweb Castle!” he said, shuddering.

“Good-bye,” suddenly the crow
said, and flew away.
The crow had seen Signor Monteverdi hiding
in the lilac bushes.

Up at one of the open windows
Flemming thought he saw a beautiful face looking out.
The beautiful face called,
"Are you from the bakery, I hope?
We are all out of bread!"

"Yes, I am from the bakery,"
Flemming Flinders lied in his teeth,
"but the bread has fallen into the water!"
The beautiful face went away, and then came out
the front door—looking sad.

"Are you a princess?" Flemming Flinders asked.

"No, we just rented the place for the summer," the girl said.

"Can I go for a ride in your boat?" she begged.

He was delighted to take her rowing.

He wanted to ask what life in Cobweb Castle
was like, but did not. The girl had
a little mandolin and played it,
plinkety-plinkety-plink.
Soon, out of nowhere, came the talented black
crow, flying over their heads.

"Here, Blackie, Blackie, Blackie!"
cried Signor Monteverdi onshore, waving his net.
"It's the Ogre of the Woods!" shouted
Flemming, but he was too late to stop
Signor Monteverdi from capturing the crow.

“Be careful, you’re tipping the boat!” cried the girl, and, indeed, they were soon floundering in the lake. The mandolin sank to the bottom and was never seen again.

“Poor crow,” the girl said. She felt like
adding, “Poor dress.” Her dress was new.
“You know, I thought the crow might
change into something,”
Flemming Flinders murmured.
They swam slowly back to the island.

On the sand they wrote their names with sticks.
Her name was Ingaborg.
Eventually the sun dried their wet clothing,
though Ingaborg's dress was never the same again.
The rowboat drifted onto some rocks.

They walked around gathering berries in baskets.
When the baskets were full, he said,
"I thought this was an enchanted forest,
but all I have met is one talking crow,
and somebody kidnapped him."
"I know, it's not like it was in the old days,"
Ingaborg sighed.
"Still, I keep thinking I am supposed to find
some money," suggested Flemming Flinders.

“Here come my mother and my father!”
exclaimed Ingaborg.
Not far off were the sounds of wild
barking and loud panting—coming closer.
Flemming imagined her parents must be
approaching on all fours.

“I guess I’ll meet them some other time,”
said Flemming, climbing quickly into the boat.
Ingaborg waved a very sad good-bye.
She would miss him, somehow.
While he rowed, far loons cried
and owls hooted in the forest.

Ingaborg's mother and father appeared,
leading on leashes some basset hounds,
which they raised for a living.
"We're sorry to have missed your new friend,"
they said, and went in the house to have tea.

Soon it was night.
Flemming Flinders walked through the forest
with only some of the moonlight
spilling through the tree-crowns.
It was very dark, so he curled up under dry bushes
and fell asleep. It was not
turning out like a fairy-tale after all.

He woke up, expecting, at least,
rubies on the ground, but there were none.
This time, he did not have
the crow to guide him, so he had to pick
his way through brambles and briars.

He arrived back at the road with his suit
torn and his hopes dashed.
“Wait till I meet that witch again,”
he declared. “I will give her a piece of my mind.”
After a while he saw Drukamella coming
down the road, holding an umbrella.
She was on her way to a garden party.

"Wait a minute!" he said, stopping her.
"I journeyed out in the world and had adventures.
I walked with the crow till I came to Cobweb Castle.
I did all the things there were to do!
Look at me now!
I'm no richer than before!
Fine witch you are!"

That made Drukamella angry.
She yelled,
"FOOLISH BOY, WHAT MADE YOU THINK I WAS A WITCH?"
She hit him over the head with her umbrella,
then hustled off down the road.

And Flemming Flinders?
He went back
to the turnips and potatoes
and started dreaming all over again.